JACK RUSSELL:
Dog Detective

Dog Den Mystery

JACK RUSSELL: Dog Detective

JACK RUSSELL: Dog Detective

Dog Den Mystery

DARREL & SALLY ODGERS

Kane Miller
A DIVISION OF EDC PUBLISHING

First American Edition 2006
by Kane/Miller Book Publishers, Inc.
La Jolla, California

First published in 2005 by Scholastic Press, Australia
Text copyright © Sally and Darrel Odgers, 2005
Cover copyright © Scholastic Australia, 2005
Cover design by Lloyd Foye & Associates
Cover photographs by Michael Bagnall
Dog, Sam, courtesy of Glenda Gould
Illustrations by Janine Dawson

For information contact:
Kane Miller, A Division of EDC Publishing
P.O. Box 470663
Tulsa, OK 74147-0663
www.kanemiller.com
www.edcpub.com

Library of Congress Control Number: 2006921535
Printed and bound in the United States of America
4 5 6 7 8 9 10

ISBN: 978-1-933605-18-0

Meet Jack Russell

Round and round and round. The paws are faster than sound. Round and round, round and round, round and …

I was running my ninety-fifth lap of the boring backyard. There was nothing else to do, except sleep in my basket and chase sparrows.

Then Sarge came home. "We're getting a transfer, Jack," he said.

Round and round and … ZOOOOP!

I skidded to a stop. I wagged my tail and did the **paw thing**. Sarge isn't the brightest biscuit in the pack, but he knew that meant —

Great! Where are we going? Is Auntie Tidge coming?

"Place called Doggeroo," said Sarge. He kicked my **squeaker bone** so it squeaked. "It'll make a change from the big city."

He was right about that.

Auntie Tidge *wasn't* coming.

I was sad about that. Auntie Tidge is Sarge's aunt. She's a big fan of mine. The day we left, she helped us pack up our things. Then she gave me a big hug.

"See you, Jackie-wackie."

Auntie Tidge is the only person alive who can call me that.

I slurped her cheek and knocked her glasses sideways. She loves it when I do that. Sarge and I went to Doggeroo in Sarge's car.

While Sarge drove, I checked scents out the window.

Jack's Facts

Cars have windows. Dogs have noses.
When these things come together,
one must be stuck out the other.
This is a fact.

 While my ears flapped, I made a **nose map**.

Jack's map:

1. Pass sausage factory.

2. Pass a yard where someone
   buried a bone last March.

3. Turn left near the house where
   someone ate chops for breakfast.

4

4. Pass a house where three cats live.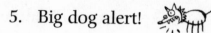

5. Big dog alert!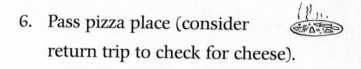

6. Pass pizza place (consider return trip to check for cheese).

7. Turn left near house with three little kids. Just the right age for dropping biscuits.

8. Pass porch with old boots.

9. Left at empty house. Suspect rats. Must check later.

Sarge turned past the empty-house-that-might-have-rats. He drove down two blocks and stopped the car.

"Here we are, Jack."

I grabbed my squeaker bone and jumped out.

I landed on an old boot that smelled of dog.

Jack's Glossary

Paw thing. *Up on hind legs, paws held together as if praying. Means pleased excitement.*

squeaker bone. *Item for exercising teeth. Not to be confused with a toy.*

Nose map. *Way of storing information collected by the nose.*

Crime Wave in Doggeroo

Jack's Facts

Boots do not belong in gardens.
Boots in gardens get chewed.
This is a fact.

I put down my squeaker bone. I grabbed Sarge's trouser leg and pulled.

"Stop that, Jack." Sarge kicked the boot aside. "No time for games."

Sarge went into the house to unpack.

I sniffed around the yard. As I sniffed, I made another nose map.

1

Jack's map:

1. Cat passed this way last Friday.

2. Corner under tree where birds often sit.

3. Strange dog buried bone here.

4. Strange dog sat here.

5. Old boot scent mixed with strange dog.

6. Strange dog scratched for fleas here.

7. Cat stalked bird here.

8. Strange dog again.

"Dinner time!" called Sarge. He put my bowl and basket out by the door.

Carefully, I put my squeaker bone into the basket. I nosed my blanket into place. (It's a good blanket. Auntie Tidge knitted it for me.) Then I ate my dinner, did what dogs do, and got into bed. I burrowed under the blanket. It smelled like Auntie Tidge.

But I didn't forget the old boot that smelled of dog.

Jack's Facts

Jack Russells (and other dogs) like to hide underneath blankets.
If we can't see you, you can't see us.
This is a fact.

I woke when the birds started singing. I got out of my basket, trotted across the grass and did what dogs do.

Then I checked my nose map.

Sniff-sniff. Sparrows-under-the-tree scent.

Sniff-sniff. Cat-crossed-the-lawn-last-night scent.

Sniff-sniff. Old-boot scent.

Sniff-sniff …

Something was wrong. I *sniff-sniffed* back a few paces. Old-boot scent. But the boot was not there.

Very strange. Very odd. Sparrows move. Cats move. Boots don't move. But why should I care? An old boot had been in my new garden. Now it wasn't. Not my problem.

I scratched at the door and yapped until Sarge let me in.

Jack's Facts

Scratching and yapping gets you into the house when you're out.
Scratching and yapping gets you out of the house when you're in.
This is a fact.

I had breakfast while Sarge got ready for work. I thought about hiding in the house. Then I remembered Sarge would be gone all morning.

I followed him outside.

"See you at lunchtime, Jack!" said Sarge.

I went back to my basket.

That's when I discovered a crime had been committed.

Someone had stolen my squeaker bone!

Jack's Facts

When someone takes an old boot,
*that's **not** my problem.*
When someone takes my squeaker bone,
*that **is** my problem.*
This is a fact.

I sniff-searched my basket. I sniff-searched the porch. I sniff-searched the yard. No squeaker bone. I sniff-searched again. No old boot. No squeaker bone.

This was serious! There was a crime wave in Doggeroo! I was glad Sarge would soon be home.

Sarge is a police detective. If someone does something bad, Sarge investigates. He finds out who did it. He finds out why they did it. He finds out how they did it. Then he stops them from doing it again.

Sarge could find out who took my squeaker bone. He could make them give it back. When Sarge came home for lunch, I laid a complaint. I grabbed his trouser leg. I tugged him towards my basket.

"No time for games now, Jack," said Sarge.

I pawed at his leg. Sarge tramped out the gate.

Sarge wasn't going to investigate the theft. Someone else would have to take the case.

Someone like: Jack Russell, Dog Detective.

And that's how I got my very first case in Doggeroo.

Meet Lord Red

"Hello, small dog!"

A face with long ears was peering over my fence. The face had big brown eyes and a shiny wet nose. The nose belonged to a big dog. It was in my **terrier-tory**.

I let my hackles rise, just a bit. I grumbled in my throat, just a bit.

Jack's Facts

Small dogs must hackle when big dogs look over their fences.
If small dogs do not hackle,
big dogs take advantage.

This is a fact.

"Who are you?" I demanded.

The big dog licked his lips. His eyebrows looked worried. "I am Uptown L-lord Setter," he stammered, "but you can c-call me 'Red.'"

"Jack Russell," I introduced myself.

"Is that your name? Or what you are?" asked the big dog.

"Both. You live around here, Red?"

"I'm from Uptown House," said Red. "I'm out walking all *alone.*"

"So?" I asked. (Could Red be a suspect in the case?)

"Caterina Smith doesn't like me to go walking *alone,*" said Red.

"Who is Caterina Smith?"

"Caterina Smith lives with me at Uptown House."

"Why doesn't she like you to go walking alone?"

"Caterina Smith thinks someone will **dognap** me."

"Why?"

Red's nose gleamed. "Caterina Smith says I'm worth a fistful of dollars. That means lots and lots."

<u>Jack's Facts</u>

*The more dollars the dog's worth,
the dimmer the dog.
This is a fact.*

I began my interview with a statement of the crime. I followed up with a direct approach.

**Interview with Lord "Red" Setter. Present:
the Suspect and Jack Russell, Dog Detective.**

"Someone stole my squeaker bone.
Someone also stole an old boot," I said. "Was
that you, Red?"

"Why should I steal a squeaker bone?"
asked Red. "I have a tug-toy. I have a snack
ball. I have a teddy bear. I have a brush. I have
a comb. I used to have a …"

"Never mind what *you* have, or used to
have," I interrupted. "If you see someone

with a squeaker bone and an old boot, bite him."

Red looked shocked. "Caterina Smith says only bad dogs bite!"

I was tired of Caterina Smith. "Don't bite, then. Come and tell me."

Red took his nose out of my terrier-tory. Then he put it back in. "Why?"

"Because whoever has them is the one who stole them."

"That's really clever, Jack!" said Red. "Maybe you'll find the ball I used to have."

Interview concluded.

I heard the click of his nails as Red trotted back up the street.

You're really thick, Red, I thought. Much too thick to be a suspect. But I didn't say so aloud.

My interview with Red showed that Red was not the thief. The thief had been sharp and sly. Red was not sharp or sly. The thief had taken my squeaker bone right out of my basket. The thief had taken the old boot, too. I hadn't heard a thing. I hadn't smelled a thing. I was ashamed.

"Call yourself a jack?" I asked myself.

"Yes," I answered myself. "Jack Russell's the name, detection's the game."

There was nothing more I could learn from the yard, so I went out.

How?

Sarge had shut the gate. There was a fence around the garden. How did I get out?

Easily.

That kind of thing doesn't matter to a jack. If a jack can get its head through a hole, the rest of the jack will follow.

Jacks dig.

Jacks jump.

Jacks burrow.

I tracked Red along the footpath. The nose map told me he had gone to the second street and turned right. Then he had trotted up the hill. At the top of the hill, I saw a house with a high fence. That must be Uptown House. So, Red had gone straight home. He hadn't been dognapped this time.

I went back to our gate. I sniff-sniffed around.

Strange dog scent. Red scent. Jack scent. Cat scent. Sparrow scent. Sarge scent.

Everything smelled the way I expected. There were no new scents that might help me catch the thief.

I went back into our yard. (Never mind how.) I went to my bowl for a snack, but I never got to eat it. *Why?*

My food had gone, and so had the bowl. So had my lovely blanket from Auntie Tidge! There had been another crime in Doggeroo.

Jack's Glossary

Terrier-tory. *The ground or land claimed by a terrier.*

Dognap. *The same as kidnap, only concerns a dog instead of a kid.*

 ## Nose to the Ground

Jack's Facts

Happy jacks are bright and breezy.
Unhappy jacks are mopey and miserable.
Angry jacks are truly terrier-fying.
This is a fact.

I lifted my lip and snarled. This thief had gone too far.

My next move was clear.

I left the yard again. (Never mind how.) I sniff-sniffed around the exit, but all I could smell was my own scent. Wait! Was that a whiff of my basket blanket?

I sniffed around. I cast about.

Strange dog scent. Cat scent. Red scent.

The Red scent went back up the street. The cat scent went across the street. The scent of my basket blanket went down the street.

I headed down the street. I followed the scent with my nose to the ground.

The paws are faster than sound when Jack Russell is nose-to-the-ground.

I tracked.

Three cats scattered. Cats know better than to sass a tracking jack.

Three **squekes** raced across the trail.

I growled.

They tucked in their tails and ran. Squekes know better than to delay a tracking jack.

I checked and cast to find the scent again.

The scent trail led to the empty-house-that-might-have-rats. That was the old place

Sarge and I had passed on our way into Doggeroo.

I squeezed through a hole in the fence. I sniffed my way up the sagging porch.

Then I heard voices. Two boys came around the corner of the empty-house-that-might-have-rats. One had a long stick for poking at things.

I crouched in the shadows of the porch until they had gone.

The door was broken. I sniffed hard, and then crawled underneath.

It was dark in the house, but I made a quick nose map.

This is what I learned:

This wasn't the empty-house-that-might-have-rats. It was the empty-house-that-**did**-have-rats.

Jack's map:

1. Rats.

2. Cat passed this way last Monday.

3. The two boys had been here before.

4. Boys had eaten a sandwich.

5. Rats had a fight over the crust.

6. More rats.

7. More rats.

8. Strange dog.

9. A whiff of my blanket. And that's not all.

10. My squeaker bone!!!

11. Old boot!!

12. Red?

Red? I sniffed around. It smelled like Red, but not quite like Red. It was the smell of a rubber ball that Red had once played with.

I sniffed my way around. It was like playing Hot and Cold.

The rat smells were strong. I wanted to hunt those rats. But where were the rats?

Maybe the boys had chased the rats away.

Maybe Red had chased the rats away.

No. The rats would have chased *Red* away. He was that sort of dog.

Maybe …

I stopped short. Jack Russell, Dog Detective, had found another clue!

It was a cache of stolen goods. Most of them smelled of dog.

Jack's Glossary

Squekes. *Small hairy dogs with bulging eyes and loud yaffles.*

# Cracking the Case?

I pounced joyfully on my squeaker bone. I gave it a good chewing. I grabbed my bowl in my teeth. I rolled on my blanket and worried it between my teeth. I …

Bad move, Jack!

What had I done?

I'd rolled on the evidence!

I'd contaminated the crime scene!

I gave myself a good talking to. Then I got on with detecting.

I had found the stolen goods. *Good.*

I hadn't caught the thief. *Bad.*

I didn't know how the thief had stolen the goods. *Bad.*

I didn't know why the thief had stolen the goods. *Bad.*

I sat down to work on my theory.

The stolen goods belonged to dogs. *Check!*

Some were mine. *Check!*

The ball was Red's. *Check!*

The old boot smelled of the strange dog that had been in our garden. *Check!*

Blanket, bowl, toys, squeaker bone, old boot.

Were those boys the thieves? Were they using stolen goods to set up a dog den in the empty house?

Why would they do that? It couldn't be for their dog. Their dog would live with them in their house.

Unless…they planned to *dognap* a dog!

Were these boys planning to dognap

Lord "Red" Setter?

Why else would they make a dog den in the empty-house-that-did-have-rats?

"You've cracked the case, Detective!" I told myself. I was sure I had found the right answer.

<u>Jack's Facts</u>

*Certain you are **right**?*
*You are probably **wrong**.*
This is a fact.

Red Again

The more I thought about it, the more sense my theory made.

Jack's Chain of Logic.

Someone had set up a dog den in the empty-house-that-had-rats.

The boys had been there.

Therefore, the boys had set up the dog den. Therefore, they would soon dognap Lord Red.

They would keep him locked in the empty house.

They would make Caterina Smith pay a fistful of dollars to get Red back.

Why did this matter to me? It wasn't my

business.

Wrong!

The dognappers had made it my business when they stole my things to put in the dog den. I began to make plans for an early arrest.

I had to let the crime go ahead. I had to catch the bad guys in the act. Then I could bark for backup (Sarge).

I had to talk to Lord Red.

I left the empty-house-that-had-had-rats and headed back towards our new house. I went up the street and turned left. Then I raced up the hill.

There was a big fence around Uptown House. Fences mean nothing to a jack on a mission.

<u>*Jack's Facts*</u>

Fences are there to be jumped over.
Fences are there to be scrambled through.

Fences are there to be burrowed under.
This is a fact.

I found a hole someone else had started digging. I crawled into it and finished the job. I stuck my nose through.

Sniff-sniff. My **super-sniffer** detected Red, so I yipped a greeting.

"Pssst! Red! Get your paws into gear and come here."

Red lollopped over. His tail was going like a propeller.

"Jack!" he yelled. "Hello, Jack! Have you come to live with me and Caterina Smith?"

Jack's Facts

If you call someone like Red quietly,
he will always bark back loudly.
This is a fact.

"Keep your bark down," I growled. "Red, you're going to be dognapped."

Red's ears went limp. He bowed down so he could see me. "W-what? When?"

"Probably tonight. In the course of my investigations, I found a dog den in the old-empty-house-that-had-rats," I said. "I believe that dog den is meant for *you.*"

"I don't need a dog den," said Red. "I live at Uptown House with Caterina

Smith. I have …"

"Never mind what you *have*," I said. "I found the ball you *used* to have. It's in the dog den. My bowl is there. So is my blanket. The dognappers have made the dog den today. Therefore they will probably dognap you tonight."

Red licked his nose. Then he looked more cheerful. He bounced. His ears bounced. His long hair bounced. "I will hide under Caterina Smith's bed," he said. "No dognapper will find me there."

"No," I said. "You must let the dognappers dognap you."

"All right," said Red. Then he asked, "Why?"

"You can't hide under a bed forever," I said. "If the dognapping goes ahead tonight, we will be ready for them. Another time, we might not be ready."

"That's really clever, Jack!" said Red. "What do I do?"

"All you have to do is let yourself be dog-napped," I said.

"All right," said Red. "How?"

I sighed. "Just let yourself get dognapped."

"All right," said Red. "I get dognapped."

"Yes. And I'll catch the dognappers. I will bark for backup. Sarge will help me arrest them."

"All right," said Red again. "How will you catch the dognappers?"

"I will be waiting on the porch of the empty-house-that-had-rats. The dognappers will drag you past me. They won't smell me. You will. I will run and bark for backup."

"So I just get myself dognapped tonight," said Red.

"That's right," I said. "You've got it."

Jack's Facts

What you tell a red setter to do is one thing.
What he **thinks** you told him to do is another
thing.
This is a fact.

I backed out of my burrow and trotted
home. I got back into the yard. (Never mind
how.) I flopped into my bare, blanketless
basket. I was just in time.

Sarge came through the gate.

"Okay, Jack?" asked Sarge. "Looks like
you've had a quiet day of it."

For a police detective, Sarge sure misses a
lot of crime.

Jack's Glossary

Super-sniffer. *Jack's nose in super-tracking mode.*

Stakeout

After dinner, Auntie Tidge called Sarge on the telephone.

"Auntie Tidge!" I yelped. I ran around, sniffing. I could hear her. I couldn't smell her.

"Doggeroo's a nice place, Auntie," I heard Sarge say. "You should come for a holiday."

A nice place? When people stole my squeaker bone and my blanket and planned to dognap red setters?

But Auntie Tidge should *definitely* come for a holiday. A long holiday.

Soon.

"You *what*?" asked Sarge. "You did *what*?

47

Look here, Auntie, you can't just ..."

I wanted to find out what Auntie Tidge had done, but it was time to go. I scratched and yapped at the door. Sarge stretched his arm and let me out.

I left the yard. (Never mind how.) I trotted up the street until I reached the fence around the empty-house-that-had-rats. Quietly, I squeezed through a hole in the fence. Quietly, I set up my stakeout.

I lay still for a long time.

It was very quiet. A few birds shuffled in the trees. A broken door banged. A couple of rats rustled and squeaked.

I wanted to hunt those rats.

I told myself a detective never gets distracted on the job. I promised the rats I would hunt them *after* we arrested the dognappers. *After* I had recovered the stolen

goods. Those goods were material evidence.
The porch could be my evidence locker.

It got darker. I strained my ears. Not a
hint of dognappers.

I sniffed the air. No fresh sniff of
dognappers. Only the scent they had left
going past the porch on their earlier visit.

I could smell that scent. And that was
odd.

I remembered the scent from the dog
den.

I did *not* remember the scent from my yard, which was the scene of the original crime.

It was a puzzle.

Question. How could the dognapper-thieves have stolen my things without leaving their scent?

Answer. They couldn't.

Conclusion. That meant they had to have an accomplice.

These questions could be answered later. Once I had set Red free, the dognappers would confess.

I kept up my stakeout. I began to get bored. I yawned.

It was dark. Where were those dognappers? Had Red let me down? Was he hiding under Caterina Smith's bed?

I shivered. I wondered if I might go to the dog den and get my blanket. Faintly, I

could smell the scent of my squeaker bone.
My jaws needed exercise. I could smell my
blanket. And Lord Red's ball. And the old
boot with the strange dog scent.

And I could smell the strange dog.

I applied my super-sniffer to the job.

The strange dog scent was stronger.

That meant the strange dog was in the
dog den.

Had the dognappers struck already?
Were they planning a wave of dognappings
all over Doggeroo?

Terrier-tory

I crawled under the door, into the empty-
house-that-had-rats.

Sniff-sniff.

The empty house wasn't empty now.
There was a dog in the dog den.

I crept forward, one paw at a time.

Question. How had I missed the dognappers?

Answer. They must have struck early,
while I was having dinner with Sarge.

All was not lost. I could brief the victim
and go back to my stakeout.

I stuck my nose into the room with the
dog den. I could smell the strange dog. My
nose twitched. The strange dog was a dirty

dog. My super-sniffer detected fleas.

These dognappers were not choosy about the class of dog they dognapped!

I crawled towards the strange dog. I was about to brief the victim when the victim bounced up and hackled.

"Who goes there?" yapped the victim. "This is *my* terrier-tory!"

"Don't panic," I told the victim briskly. "Detective Jack Russell is on the case."

"Gerrofff!" yapped the victim. "Geddout

of here before I bite your sniffer off!"

I could see now that the victim was a fox terrier. More or less. He was mostly black and white, with dirty blotches. His hackles were up.

"Halt!" I said. (My own hackles were trying to rise, but I forced them down.) "Back off before I am forced to bite you!"

"You and whose army?' sneered the victim. The more-or-less fox terrier bared his teeth. "Geddoff my patch!"

"Fine, if you don't *want* to be rescued," I sniffed.

I backed off a bit.

Jack's Facts

If a terrier bares its teeth, it means business. If a terrier means business, it's time to back off.

Even if you, too, are a terrier.
This is a fact.

"Rescued!" yapped the victim. "That's a laugh! Go back to your basket, you nosy jack."

"What do *you* know about my basket?" I demanded.

The fox terrier looked me in the eye. Out of the corner of *my* eye, I saw his front paw sneaking sideways. He was trying to scratch something out of sight.

That something was my blanket. That's when it hit me. This victim wasn't a *victim*. This victim was the *criminal*!

"You haven't been dognapped," I said.

It wasn't a question. It was a fact.

"Back off, Jack," snarled Foxie. "This is *my* terrier-tory."

"So you said before," I said. "But you've been on *my* terrier-tory, haven't you? You've been stealing my things."

Foxie gave up trying to hide the blanket. He put his front paw on my squeaker bone. "Serves you right," he muttered. "*You* moved in on *my* terrier-tory first."

"Dogwash!" I said.

Foxie shuddered. "Don't say the 'wash' word!" he snarled. "You and that human moved in on my place."

"Dogwash!" I said again. Then I remembered something. "That old boot is yours."

"Right," snarled Foxie. "When you stole my terrier-tory, I had to move on." He sniffed. "Story of my life."

"So," I said. "You used to live alone in my yard. You don't have a human landlord. You are a street dog."

The fox terrier narrowed his eyes. "Wanna make something of it?"

"Sarge and I moved in, so you moved on," I continued. "But you came back for your old boot."

"A dog's got a right to his own old boot," said Foxie.

"A dog *doesn't* have a right to my squeaker bone, my blanket, my bowl, my dinner and Lord Red's ball!" I countered. "Foxie, I am arresting you ..."

I broke off.

Why did I break off?

Because I'd solved the case of the Doggeroo Dog Den, but I couldn't make an arrest.

Sarge would arrest dognappers. Sarge would not arrest a homeless foxie.

What could I do now? What *should* I do

now? I had a problem.

While I was pondering my problem, I heard **pan-dog-monium** outside.

Jack's Glossary

Pan-dog-monium. *A lot of noise that involves dogs.*

# Dogged by Disaster

I heard yells. I heard barks. I heard yaffles. I heard Lord Red.

"Stay there," I said to Foxie.

I left the dog den. I streaked out of the empty-house-that-had-rats. I shot through the hole in the fence. I skidded to a halt.

Lord "Red" Setter was galloping down the street. His ears were flying. His tail was streaming in the moonlight. He was howling, "Come and get meeeee!"

Behind Lord Red ran a woman.

She was yelling, "Lordie! Lordie! Come here. Lordeeeee!"

Behind the woman ran three other people,

and three squekes.

The people were yelling, "What's going on?"

and

"Stop!"

and

"Don't you know what *time* it is?"

and

"That dog should be tied up!"

The squekes were yaffling the way
squekes do.

Behind the squekes ran Sarge. He spotted me. "There you are, Jack! I was wondering where you'd got to."

Was I pleased to see Sarge!

I gave him the paw thing and then launched myself into the air. (They don't call us Jumping Jacks for nothing.) Sarge caught me. Now I was higher than Red and higher than the squekes. That made me the dominant dog.

"Stop in the name of the paw!" I barked.

The squekes stopped yelping and whined. Red stopped howling and crouched down.

"What *are* you doing?" I barked.

"Sorry, Jack," said Red. "I tried to get myself dognapped the way you said. But no one would dognap me."

"I *said*, to *let* yourself be dognapped, not to

get yourself dognapped!" I snapped.

"Oh, sorry." Red crouched lower. "My mistake." His tongue lolled in the moonlight.

The woman (who was Caterina Smith) grabbed him by the collar. "Lordie, how *could* you be so naughty?"

Lord Red whined and pawed at Caterina Smith's leg.

The squekes started yaffling again.

Everyone yelled at them to be quiet.

I drooped in Sarge's arms.

There were no dognappers after Lord Red.

The thief was only a street dog.

The dog den was only the street dog's new lair.

I had got it wrong all down the line.

My first case seemed dogged by disaster.

Things quietened down at last. The squekes

and the other three people went home.

Caterina Smith explained to Sarge that her dog had run away.

Sarge explained to Caterina Smith that his dog had also run away.

Sarge and Caterina Smith frowned at Lord Red and me.

Then I had an idea.

Jack's Facts

Jack Russells are very good at having ideas.
When a jack has an idea, it works.
Mostly.
This is a fact.

My idea was this. Now Sarge was here, he could help me take my belongings back to our place! They were still evidence of a crime, but I had gone off the idea of arresting Foxie.

I did a quick **jack-knife** and shot out of Sarge's arms. I hit the ground running.

I shot through the hole in the fence. I streaked into the empty-house-that-had-rats. I raced back into the dog den.

Red fled after me.

That is, Red *tried* to flee after me. It wasn't my fault Red got stuck in the fence.

I half thought the thief would have left the scene, but he was still there. He was sitting on the dirty floor with his chin on his old boot.

I stared at Foxie.

Foxie stared back. He licked his lips.

"Well?" asked Foxie. "You going to push me out of this terrier-tory too?"

I thought about that. It didn't seem fair

to move Foxie on again.

"Look ..." we both said together. We stopped.

"Look," I said again. "Suppose you give back my things. And give Lord Red back his ball. You can keep the old boot."

"That's big of you," muttered Foxie.

"Then you can keep this terrier-tory and I'll keep mine," I said. "Just don't steal anything else."

Foxie sulked. "It's a dog's life," he complained. "If I don't steal, I don't eat."

I thought about that. While I was thinking, I heard Sarge pushing through the broken door.

"*Now* look what you've done!" snapped Foxie. He grabbed his old boot in his jaws. "You've got *people* coming here. People have sticks. People hate dogs like me ... "

"It's only Sarge … " I began, but I was half wrong.

It *was* Sarge, but it wasn't *only* Sarge.

Sarge came in, flashing a big torch. Behind him came Caterina Smith and Red. Red's coat was all messed up where he'd got stuck in the fence. Behind *them* came …

"Auntie Tidge!" I yelped. I shot across the floor and launched myself into the air. (They don't call us Jumping Jacks for nothing.)

Auntie Tidge caught me. (She's had a lot of practice.) "Who's a lovely boy then, Jackie-wackie?"

Foxie gave me a look under his eyebrows. *"Jackie-wackie?"*

"Call me that and die," I snarled. I gave Auntie Tidge a big slurp up the cheek and knocked her glasses sideways. She loves it when I do that.

And that's when I had my best idea ever. Suddenly everything was clear ... I knew *exactly* what had to happen to bring my first case to a **successful conclusion**.

Jack's Glossary

Jack-knife. *A kind of sudden leap and twist performed by jacks when they want to get down in a hurry.*

Successful conclusion. *An ending where everything turns out properly. The stolen goods are returned to their owners. The thief is reformed. The detective is proud of his work.*

 # Foxie Reformed?

Foxie was trying to slink away. I put a stop to that by jack-knifing out of Auntie Tidge's arms.

I raced after Foxie and put my paw on the back of his head.

"Get your head *down,*" I hissed. "Pretend you're a nice dog down on his luck."

Foxie started to growl. I slurped him across the chops. The growl turned into a gurgle. I whacked my tail as hard as I could. I pushed Foxie's head down on the floor.

"I'll get you for this, Jack Russell!" gurgled Foxie.

"Shut up!" I said. "*Nice* dog, remember." I

scratched at my side as Foxie's fleas began to move.

Just as I planned, Auntie Tidge and Sarge came to see what I was doing.

Just as I planned, Auntie Tidge bent down and peered at Foxie.

"You poor doggie!" said Auntie Tidge. She pushed me gently away from Foxie. "Poor, darling little doggie!"

Foxie had been glaring at me. Now he glared at Auntie Tidge instead.

But not for long. Nobody glares at Auntie Tidge for long.

Foxie's glare turned into a gleam. He caught my eye.

"*Do it!*" I ordered, scratching at my neck. "*Nice* dog. Auntie Tidge has *biscuits*."

Foxie wagged his tail. It was so long since that tail had wagged I think I heard it creaking.

That did it. Auntie Tidge hoisted Foxie into her arms. "I'm taking this poor little fellow home," she said.

"You can't do that, Auntie!" said Sarge. "You know your landlord won't let you have a dog."

"That's all right," said Auntie Tidge. "Didn't I tell you? I've decided to come and live in Doggeroo!"

That was the end of my first case. Auntie Tidge carried Foxie (and the old boot) off to give him a bath.

"I'll get you for this, Jack Russell!" hollered Foxie.

"You already did!" I yapped back. "I'll be chasing fleas for hours!"

Sarge helped me gather up my blanket, my squeaker bone and my bowl, and we all set off for home. And that was just about that. Except …

Lord Red suddenly pulled away from Caterina Smith. He pounced on the rubber ball. "You're a really clever detective, Jack!" said Red.

"Thanks," I said. I scratched my ear. "But I got it wrong. There weren't any dognappers after all."

"Who cares?" asked Red. "You found my favorite ball!"

Jack's Facts

Dogs chase fleas because fleas chase dogs. This is a fact.

About the Authors

Darrel and Sally Odgers live in Tasmania with their Jack Russell terriers, Tess, Trump, Pipwen, Jeanie and Preacher, who compete to take them for walks. They enjoy walks, because that's when they plan their stories. They toss ideas around and pick the best. They are also the authors of the popular *Pet Vet* series.

PET VET The new series from the authors of Jack Russell: Dog Detective!

Meet Trump! She's an A.L.O., or Animal Liaison Officer. She works with Dr. Jeanie, the young vet who runs Pet Vet Clinic in the country town of Cowfork. Dr. Jeanie looks after animals that are sick or injured. She also explains things to the owners. But what about the animals? Who will tell them what's going on? That's where Trump comes in.

JACK RUSSELL:
Dog Detective

Read all of Jack's adventures!

Jack Russell:
the detective with
a nose for crime.